Andréa Barros
illustrated by Thalita Dol

Heart-Shaped Friendship

HEART-SHAPED FRIENDSHIP

©2020 Andréa Barros
All rights reserved.
Written by Andréa Barros
Illustration and design Thalita Dol
Editor John Matthew Fox of Bookfox

Barros, Andréa
HEART-SHAPED FRIENDSHIP
1ª ed. - Vancouver: Andréa Barros, 2020

ISBN: 978-1-7771259-0-5 Hardcover
ISBN: 978-1-7771259-1-2 Paperback
ISBN: 978-1-7771259-2-9 Ebook
ISBN: 978-1-7771259-3-6 Hardcover (Portuguese)
ISBN: 978-1-7771259-5-0 Paperback (Portuguese)
ISBN: 978-1-7771259-4-3 Ebook (Portuguese)

1. Children 5-8 years 2. Friendship 3. Empathy 4. Trisomy 21 5. Down syndrome 6. Limitations 7. Differences 8. Fear 9. Speech delay 10. Cognitive delay

Gratitude

To my Higher Power, who gives meaning to my life.

To my family, who nourishes me with unconditional love.

To you, who opened this book and your heart to a world of love and empathy.

Andrea Barrios

Dear Kelly & Family
Be Kind
Be Brave
Spread Love

Andrea Barrios.

On the first day of school, my hands were sweating as I walked toward Henry Hudson Elementary School.

Dad was too busy on his phone to notice.

She quickly got up and said with a funny smile,

Ooo... Eee...

I looked puzzled, and her mom explained. "She means *sorry*. Summy's so excited for her first day at school with Mrs. Mel!"

I said, "I'm in Mrs. Mel's class too."

Her mom gave a big smile.
"Great! What's your name?"

I replied, "Hope."

Summy repeated my name
in her own way.

"Ow."

Then she stared at my heart-shaped necklace.

I guess we both love hearts because she was wearing a dress with colorful hearts printed on it. She left the scooter behind and held my hand as we walked toward the classroom.

People were staring, probably because of Summy's funny smile.

After we said goodbye to our parents, I thought, *She could be my best friend even though she can't pronounce my name.*

In the classroom, Mrs. Mel asked us to sit in a circle and say our names.

When it was Summy's turn, she said, "Me."

So, I shouted, "No, her name is SUMMY!"

She frowned and said in a bossy way, "Yeah, ME!"

Mrs. Mel said Summy would need our help to learn full words. She announced a special competition.

"Everybody will teach Summy one word. Then, when everyone succeeds, we will have a Popsicle party!"

We all got excited and screamed.

Summy licked her little finger and smiled!
She must love Popsicles as much as we do!

At recess, everyone was crowded around Summy, teaching her words. Valentina was the first one to have a shot. She kicked the ball toward Summy and said, "Ball."

Summy grabbed the ball and shouted, "MINE!"
Valentina shook her head and explained.
"No, it's ours to share. But If you wanna play, you must say BALL!"

So, Summy said, "Ball!"

Valentina looked to the crowd and punched the air!
"Yes, I can be a soccer coach when I grow up!"

Then, Bunny taught Summy the word *bonbon* by asking her to choose between a small chocolate candy and a big one.

Summy said *bonbon* twice and ate both. Bunny didn't find it funny at all.

Suddenly Danny showed up, singing and making strange moves.
"*Oh, I'm a chummy boy. Yes, I'm a funny boy.*
Oh, I'm a yummy, tummy, funny, lucky, gummy boy.
Chummy, funny, chummy, funny, famous boy!"

Summy's almond-shaped eyes went round. She laughed loudly, watching Danny's pink cheeks turn to red.
Then she said, "Boy!"

She clapped her hands, and Danny shouted, "Yes, I can be a superstar when I grow up!"

Back in the classroom, Mrs. Mel had a colorful board on the wall in a shape of a Popsicle. On it she wrote words that other kids had already taught Summy.

I was so impressed! I had to choose my own word, and I knew exactly what it would be, *heart!* I'm gonna teach her the word *heart*!

I ran toward Summy and said, "HEART. Repeat after me. Heart."

She smiled, and opened and closed her mouth, but no sound came out of it!

I repeated the word a few times, and the same thing happened over and over.

"H-E-A..." I decided to spell it. No luck. I didn't know how to spell it! So I said it slowly. "H...e...a...r...t."
And fast. "HEART!"

She laughed.

Maybe she had learned too many words for the day, but I would not give up!

During the following weeks, Summy and I would always see each other at school

and on playdates.

She introduced me to her dog, Bro –short for Brother– and taught me that dogs from Brazil say AU AU instead of WOOF WOOF.

Then she would jump on my back, and we would pretend to be Bro's buddy, mimicking him.

I kept trying to teach Summy the word *heart*, but she wasn't learning it. I tried everything. I drew it, I sang it, I chanted it.

But no matter what I did, she wouldn't say it. She would just make the sign for heart.

Even though I loved Summy, I wanted to cry. All my hard work wasn't paying off.

By this time the other kids had already taught Summy a word, and I started getting strange looks from them.

I was letting the group down. That's exactly what Pandora told me one day on the bottom of the slide.

"Come on, Hope, everyone is afraid we won't have our Popsicle party because of you!"
I said, "I'm trying...!"

"I know... It's not your fault! My parents told me *everything* about kids like her."
And I said, "What?"

"Haven't you noticed anything different about Summy?"

I replied in a blink of an eye. "Oh, yes! She doesn't have a front tooth! And guess what?! It never came out!"

Pandora slapped her forehead and rolled her eyes. Suddenly Summy came out from the back of the slide. By the sad look she gave us before running away, I could tell our words had hurt her.

I ran around the school searching for Summy, but she was nowhere to be seen.

When I got to the big kid's playground, I heard voices. "OW, HELP! *Tiii!*"

Summy was stuck on the top step of the climbing wall! I didn't think twice. I had to rescue her!

So I started to climb the wall, even though it was super hard. I had to get there quickly to rescue my bestie. There was a big group of kids gathered close to the wall, and I overheard them talking as I was climbing.

"How did she get there in the first place? She's so little!"

"I don't know, dude. I've been trying to climb this wall for ages!"

Once I got up high, I noticed Summy had skinned her right knee. She was scared because there was a lot of blood. I had a plan to get us down and told Summy, "Let's play dog, okay?"

So, she jumped on my back and slowly we climbed down toward the ground. I had a hard time keeping focused because Summy was licking my neck like Bro!

The kids clapped and cheered for us when we reached the bottom!

I was brave enough to look at Summy and say, "Sorry, I didn't mean to hurt your feelings."

Then she smiled, and I was so happy to see her smiling again that nothing else mattered anymore.

"You're my best friend, and that's more precious than any word or any Popsicle party."

She carefully drew the heart shape on my chest, one time, two times, and then three times.

Then she opened her mouth and, to my surprise, said: "Love."

For the first time in my life, I cried and smiled at the same time.

The next morning, Mrs. Mel announced our Popsicle board was complete. We won the challenge!

She thanked everyone for their hard work.

Then I got up and told them about the new word on the board.

"Actually, I didn't teach Summy a word. She taught me. Summy taught me that *heart* means *love*. That people closest to our heart are the people we love. She's my best friend, and even though she doesn't speak many words, she taught me that love can move us! Now, I feel I'm special, like Summy!"

Mrs. Mel was smiling with tears in her eyes and said, "Hope, it's good to have you around."

Then we heard the ice cream truck's melody and ran out to the playground.

Our party was about to start!

ANDRÉA BARROS grew up in Recife, Brazil, and lived in Australia and Germany before moving to Vancouver.

Parachuting, working on a crocodile farm, and swimming in dangerous waters with husband-to-be set her up for the most fulfilling adventure in life–raising her daughters Skye and Summer.

As a mother of a child with Trisomy 21, she learned everything is possible when you let LOVE guide your life. Andréa believes experiences must be shared to help others, and this book is just the beginning of a beautiful journey.

andreabarros.com
@andreabarros.author

THALITA DOL is also Brazilian, a beach lover born in Rio de Janeiro. She moved from forever-sunny Rio to beautiful Vancouver with her husband and two daughters. She wouldn't have it any other way, and now loves life in all four seasons.

She started drawing when she learned how to hold a pencil, and has been drawing ever since. She had fun illustrating for school books, children's magazines, fabric patterns and even backgrounds for animated movies. But story books are her favorites and she hopes you have enjoyed what she created for this one!

On her free time, Thalita enjoys going on outings with her family, creating baby dolls and sewing dresses for her daughters.

thalitadol.com
thalitadolillustration

Lightning Source UK Ltd.
Milton Keynes UK
UKHW051159301220
375905UK00007BA/88